For
Brian and Sarah
with love

RL

For
Helen and Lucy

SL

First published by Candlewick Press

CANDLEWICK PRESS
2067 MASSACHUSETTS AVENUE
CAMBRIDGE MA 02140

ISBN 0-590-67983-X

Text copyright © 1994 by Reeve Lindbergh.
Illustrations copyright © 1994 by Stephen Lambert.
All rights reserved. Published by Scholastic Inc., 555 Broadway,
New York, NY 10012, by arrangement with Candlewick Press.

12 11 10 9 8 7 6 5 4 3 2 1   6 7 8 9/9 0 1/0

Printed in the U.S.A.   08

First Scholastic printing, May 1996

What Is the Sun?

Reeve Lindbergh   illustrated by Stephen Lambert

CANDLEWICK PRESS
CAMBRIDGE, MASSACHUSETTS

What is the sun?

The sun is a star.

Is the sun near?   *No, it is far.*

What does it do?

It sends light down to you.

Like my lamp, only higher?
More like a big fire.

Can I see it at night?
No, you see the moonlight.

The moon is a star?

Not a star, just a place.

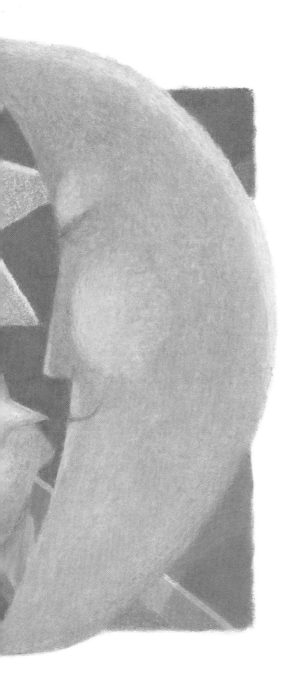

Why does it smile?

It looks like a face.

Sometimes thin, sometimes fat?

Yes, the moon is like that.

Does it shine in the day?

No, it just fades away.

What else does it do?

It pulls the tides, too.

What are the tides?

The whole moving sea.

With the fish, and the whales?
Yes, definitely.

Where do tides go?

Up and down, ebb and flow.

On the beach where I play?
Up and down, night and day.

Tides go out and go in?
Like your breath, and the wind.

What is the wind?

Wind is air, blowing air.

Where does it blow?

Through the world, everywhere.

The wind comes and goes?

It goes right through your nose!

But that can be cold!

When deep winter takes hold.

Is wind ever warm?
In a summer rainstorm.

What is the rain?
The rain makes things grow.

Like the flowers and trees?

And the rivers that flow.

Where does it rain?

On the sea, hill, and plain.

And it rains on my head?

Not when you're here in bed!

And after the rain?

Then the earth's green again.

What is the earth?

It's our home—a big ball.

With the sun and the moon?

And the raindrops that fall.

And the wind and the tides?
And the people, besides.

Even children, like me?
Everybody you see.

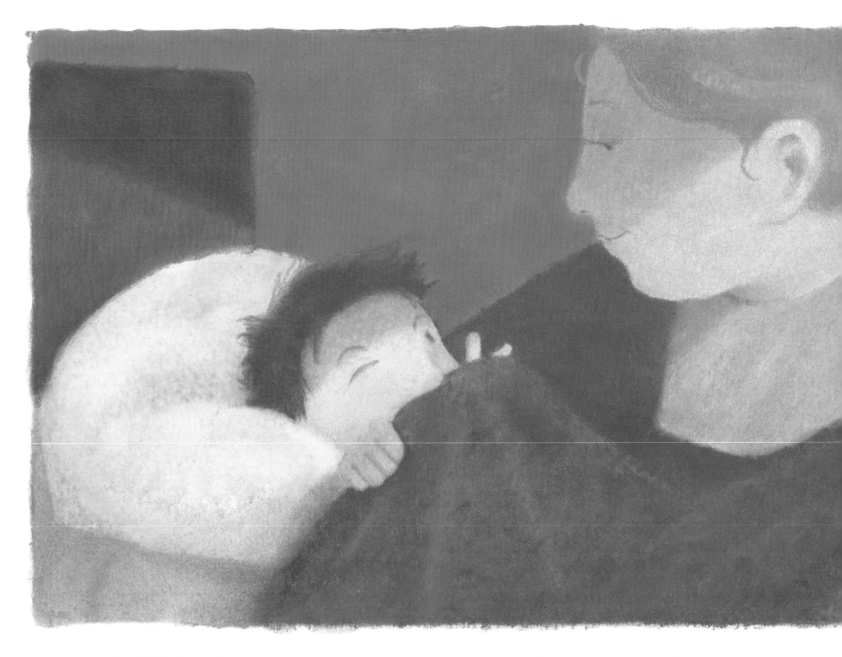

So you'll be here too?   *Yes, forever, with you.*

Then I think it's all right. *I love you.... Good night.*